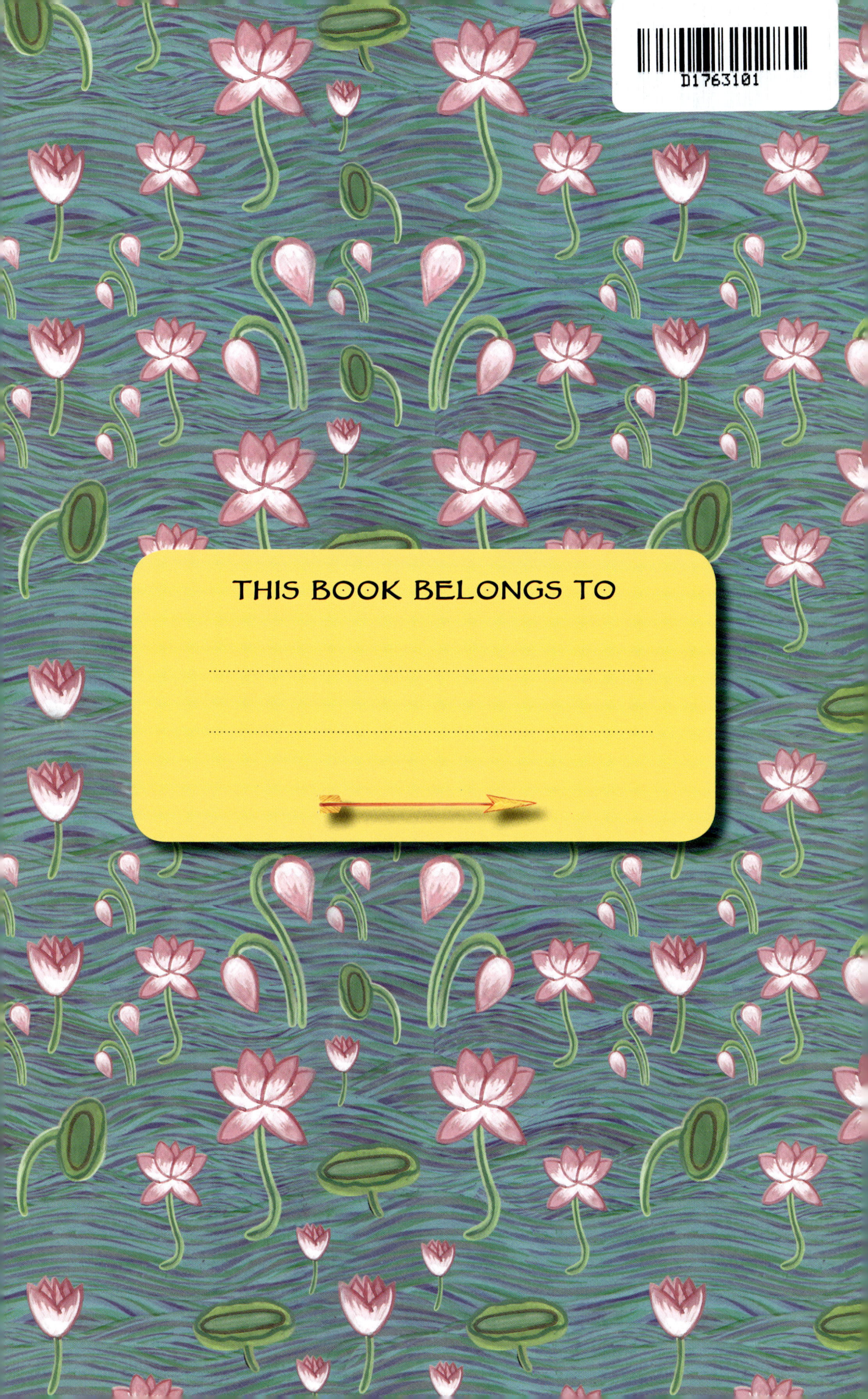

THE MAHABHARATA
CHILDREN'S ILLUSTRATED CLASSICS

DRONACHARYA *and* HIS DISCIPLES

Retold by **CHARU AGARWAL DHANDIA**
Art **KAVITA SINGH KALE** *Design* **RACHITA RAKYAN**

Published by
Rupa Publications India Pvt. Ltd 2020
7/16, Ansari Road, Daryaganj
New Delhi 110002

Sales centres:
Allahabad Bengaluru Chennai
Hyderabad Jaipur Kathmandu
Kolkata Mumbai

Edition copyright © Rupa Publications Pvt. Ltd 2020

All rights reserved.
No part of this publication may be reproduced, transmitted,
or stored in a retrieval system, in any form or by any means, electronic, mechanical, photocopying,
recording or otherwise,
without the prior permission of the publisher.

ISBN: 978-81-291-4971-8

First impression 2020

10 9 8 7 6 5 4 3 2 1

The moral right of the author has been asserted.

Printed at Nutech Print Services - India

This book is sold subject to the condition that it shall not, by way of trade or otherwise, be lent, resold, hired out, or otherwise circulated, without the publisher's prior consent, in any form of binding or cover other than that in which it is published.

Charu Agarwal Dhandia weaves together her two biggest passions—studying Indian classical literature and creative storytelling. She is an economist by training and works in the social development space.

Kavita Singh Kale's background as an artist and a designer enables her to draw a thin line between design following functionality and pure self-expression. This has helped her evolve as a transmedia artist. Her work includes art installations, children's books, comics, paintings and videos.

Rachita Rakyan combines over 15 years of expertise in graphic design and art direction with deep understanding of functionality and aesthetics across print, publishing, branding and digital media.

CONTENTS

KURU DYNASTY	*IV-V*
KEY CHARACTERS	*VI-VII*
DRONACHARYA'S TEST	1
EKALAVYA	11
KARNA AND RADHA	23
THE COMPETITION	29
DRONACHARYA AND DRUPADA	41

KURU DYNASTY

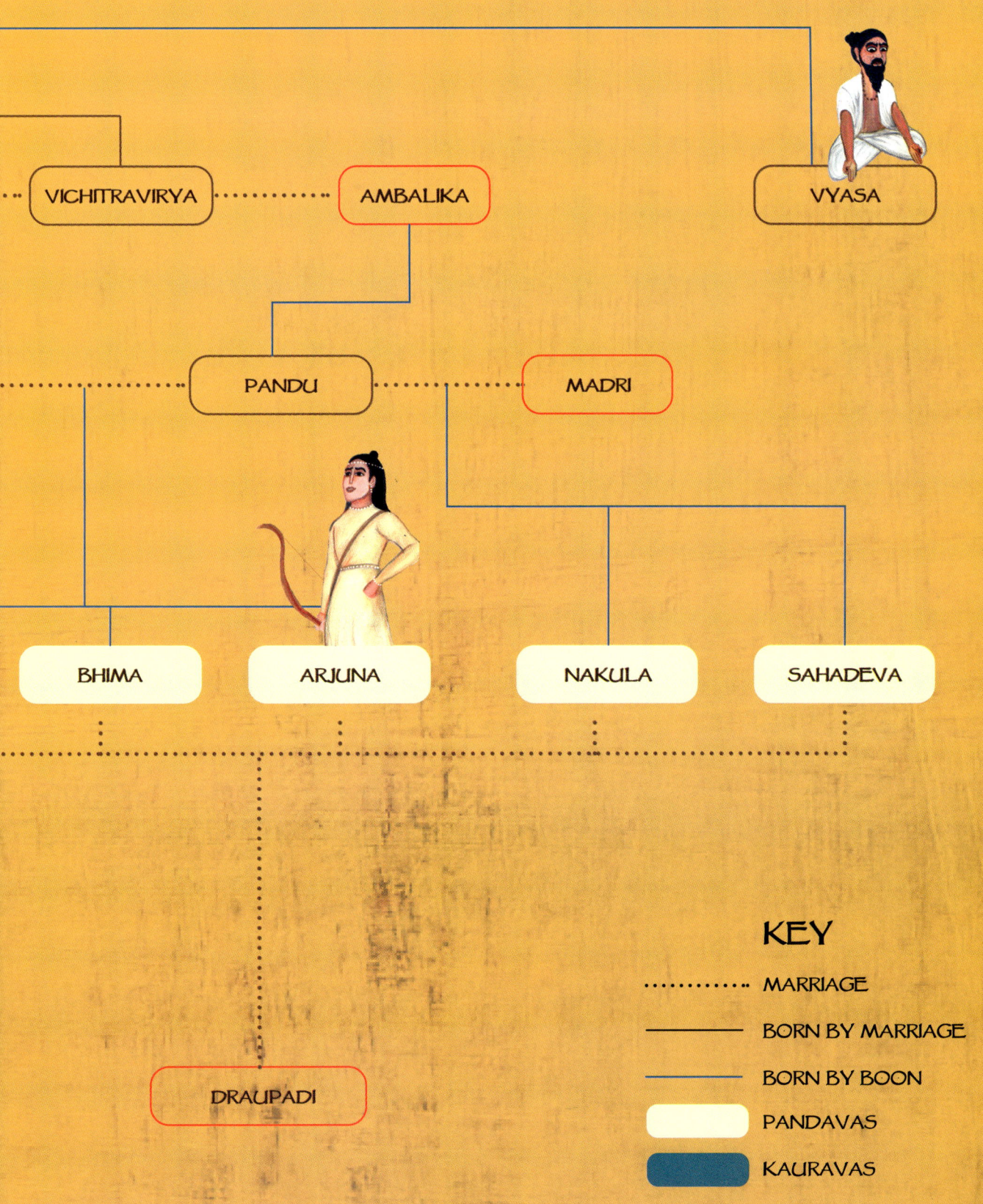

KEY CHARACTERS

ARJUNA

Arjuna was the third of the Pandava brothers born to Kunti by the boon of Lord Indra. He was the greatest archer in the country. Arjuna was Dronacharya's favourite pupil.

DURYODHANA

Duryodhana was the eldest brother amongst the Kauravas and born to princess Gandhari as a blessing from sage Vyasa. He was very jealous of the Pandavas.

DRUPADA

Drupada was the King of Panchala and the childhood friend of Dronacharya. He performed a great yagna and became the father of Draupadi and Dhristadhyumna who emerged from the fire.

DRONACHARYA

Dronacharya was guru to the Pandava and the Kaurava princes while they were growing up in Hastinapur. Although Dronacharya loved all the princes, he was most fond of Arjuna. Dronacharya married Kripi and was the father of Ashwatthama.

KARNA

Karna was born to young Kunti by the boon of Lord Surya. He was raised by a charioteer Adhiratha and his wife Radha. Later, he became a supremely skilled archer known for his loyalty and friendship with Duryodhana.

EKALAVYA

Ekalavya was a young prince of the Nishadas and aspired to learn archery from the great Dronacharya. Though Dronacharya refused to train him, Ekalavya continued to worship him as his guru and displayed great devotion and dedication towards Dronacharya.

The Pandavas and Kauravas were learning archery and warrior skills from their guru Dronacharya. They learnt to use weapons, aim arrows and use various *astras*.

Dronacharya loved all his students. But Arjuna was his favourite. He was a sincere and obedient student, and a keen learner.

Arjuna practised day and night. Dronacharya was certain that he would become the greatest warrior in Hastinapur.
One day, Dronacharya wanted to test the princes. He made a small wooden sparrow and hung it from the branch of a jamun tree.

Dronacharya called the princes and said, 'Look at that bird hanging from the tree. The target is to hit the eye of the bird. Not an inch here or there, but straight at the eye! Let me see who is the best archer of you all.'
The princes got their bows and arrows ready.

First, Dronacharya called Yudhishthira and asked, 'Yudhishthira, what do you see?'

Yudhishthira thought for a moment and said, 'I see the sparrow's body and my brothers.'

Dronacharya was disappointed. He said, 'Go back. You will not be able to do it.'

Then he called Duryodhana. 'Duryodhana, what do you see?' he asked.
Duryodhana looked up and said, 'I see the bird, the tree, and you, my dear guru.'
Dronacharya shook his head disappointedly and said, 'Go back!'
One after the other, the princes failed.

Finally, it was Arjuna's turn. Dronacharya asked, 'Arjuna, what do you see?'
'I only see the eye of the bird,' Arjuna replied.
Dronacharya was very happy. This was the answer he was waiting for.
Then Arjuna aimed and shot right at the bird's eye.

Dronacharya hugged Arjuna in joy and said, 'Princes, you can be successful only if you concentrate on your task. All of you were distracted by the things around you. Arjuna could see only the bird's eye because he concentrated fully on the target. You should be like him.'

EKALAVYA

Prince Ekalavya was the son of the King of the Nishadas. Ekalavya's dream was to learn archery from the great Dronacharya. He spent years practising so that Dronacharya would not refuse to train him.

One morning, Dronacharya was walking in his garden. He saw a young boy walking towards him. Ekalavya bowed to Dronacharya and said, 'O Guru, you are the greatest archer in the world. Please make me your student.'

Dronacharya replied, 'I train only royal princes. I cannot teach you. However, you have my blessings to become a great warrior, my child.'

Ekalavya's eyes filled with tears. He went away, disappointed. But he did not lose hope. He collected some clay and made an idol of Dronacharya.

From that day on, he practised archery in front of the idol of his guru. With each passing day, Ekalavya became more and more skilled.

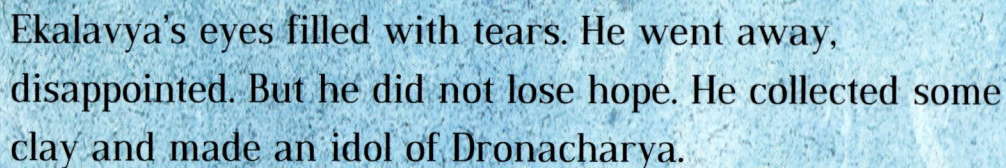

One afternoon, Dronacharya and the princes went hunting in the forest. Suddenly, a stray dog started barking. This interrupted Ekalavya in his practice. He picked his bow and shot some arrows at the dog's mouth.

The princes saw this and were amazed at how skilfully Ekalavya shot the arrows without hurting the dog. Dronacharya said, 'This is certainly the work of a great archer! Let's look for him!' Soon, they found Ekalavya practising under a tree.

Seeing his guru in front of him, Ekalavya fell at Dronacharya's feet in respect and devotion. Dronacharya looked at Ekalavya and asked, 'Who has trained you so well?'

Overjoyed, Ekalavya replied, 'All this while, I have been practising in front of you, my guru.' Ekalavya pointed at the clay idol of Dronacharya.
Dronacharya was speechless! He was touched by Ekalavya's devotion. But he wanted to test him.

Dronacharya said, 'If I am your guru, you must give me my *gurudakshina*.' With folded hands, Ekalavya said, 'Dear Guru, I owe everything to you. I am ready to give you anything you want.'

'Then, give me the thumb of your right hand!' said Dronacharya.

The next moment, Ekalavya cut his thumb, knelt down and placed it at his guru's feet.

This act of obedience deeply humbled Dronacharya. From that day onwards, Ekalavya became known for his devotion towards his guru Dronacharya.

KARNA AND RADHA

It was Karna's sixteenth birthday. He sat quietly in a corner of the house. Stroking his hair, his mother Radha asked, 'What is troubling you, my son?'

Karna said, 'Father gifted me a beautiful chariot and horses on my birthday. But I don't want to be a charioteer. I want to become an archer, Mother! I spend all my time with my bows and arrows. I yearn to be an archer! Tell me Mother, why do I feel this way?'

Radha's eyes filled with tears. She said, 'Son, let me tell you a story. It will answer all your questions.'

Radha began narrating her story.
One morning, your father Adhiratha had gone to the river for his daily bath. Suddenly, he saw a wooden basket floating down the river. There was a beautiful baby boy sleeping in it.

He wore bright golden armour and lovely golden earrings. Adhiratha brought the baby home. Deep in our hearts, we knew that God had sent this beautiful baby to us in answer to our prayers. From that day, we lived together happily as a family.

Radha hugged Karna and said, 'That child was you Karna! You are not a charioteer's son. You are meant to be a Kshatriya, a warrior!'

Karna flung his arms around Radha and cried, 'Bless me, Mother! I want to become the best archer the world has ever seen!'

THE COMPETITION

Back in Hastinapur, King Dhrithrashtra and Vidura announced a tournament for the royal princes. People from all over the country were invited to the grand event at the palace. The day of the tournament came and hundreds of people gathered in the arena.

Soon, it was Arjuna's turn. He walked to the middle of the arena and bowed in respect to his grandfather Bhishma and uncle Dhrithrashtra. He began his spectacular play with arrows. He created fire with one arrow and a spring of water with another. People watched, amazed and enchanted.

Suddenly, everyone's attention was caught by a young man walking into the arena. It was Karna. He walked up to Arjuna and said, 'I challenge you, Arjuna!'
There was a murmur in the crowd.

Karna picked up his bow and started shooting his arrows with remarkable skill. The crowd cheered loudly.

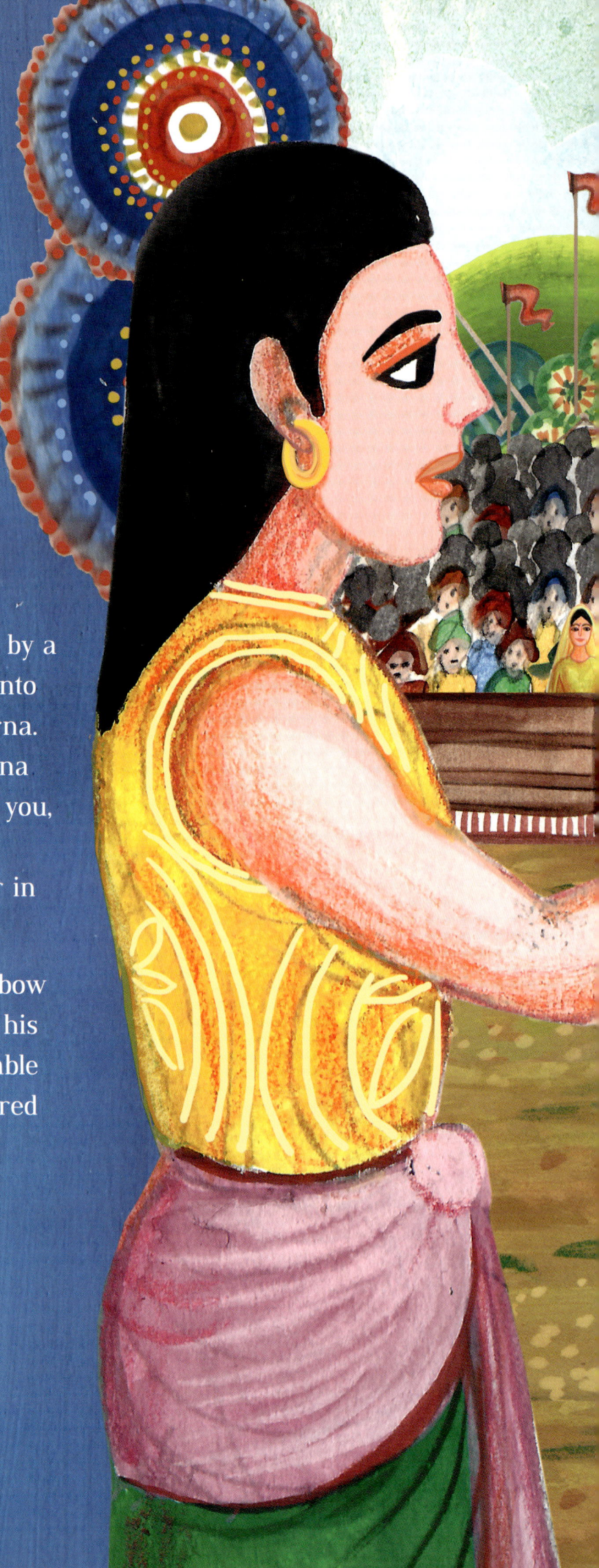

At this moment, Karna's father Adhiratha entered the arena and embraced him. Kripacharya, the master archer, announced, 'This competition is meant only for royal princes. Karna is not a prince. He cannot challenge Arjuna!'

Duryodhana had been observing Karna and was greatly impressed by his talent. He came up to Karna and said, 'I declare Karna the ruler of Anga from this moment. He can now participate in this competition!'

Karna was overjoyed and touched. He said, 'Duryodhana, thank you for this great honour. It means a lot to me.' Duryodhana smiled and said, 'You are a very skilled archer, Karna. Everyone should appreciate your talent!'

Duryodhana and Karna embraced each other. From that day, they both became great friends and promised to support each other all their lives.

Night fell and Duryodhana took Karna in his chariot. They rode away together from the arena celebrating their new friendship.

DRONACHARYA AND DRUPADA

One morning, Dronacharya called the princes and said, 'I have called all of you for something important. You all have been wonderful students. It is now time for me to ask for my *gurudakshina*.'

The princes spoke together, 'Guru, you can ask us for anything! We owe everything to you!'

Dronacharya said, 'I do not need wealth, I need your loyalty. Let me tell you a story.'

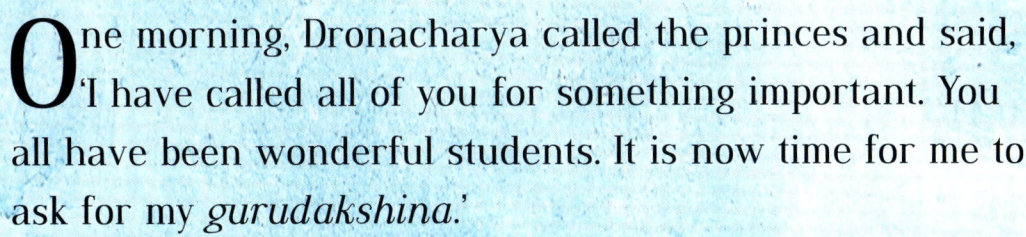

Dronacharya began narrating the story of King Drupada to the princes.

Many years ago, King Drupada and I were students of the great guru Bharadwaja. Together, we learnt the art of archery. During this time, we became very good friends. One day, Drupada said, "Dronacharya, my friend, the day I become a King, I promise to share my kingdom with you."

Years later, Drupada became the King of Panchala and I visited him to ask for help. To my disbelief, he insulted me in front of everyone and asked me to leave. His behaviour hurts me even today.

Drupada's insult to their guru made the princes angry. They said, 'We will capture Drupada and bring him to you!' So, an army was formed and in a few days, the princes left for Panchala.

First, the Kauravas went ahead and attacked the palace. Drupada was a great archer and easily defeated the Kauravas. It was now the turn of the Pandavas to lead the charge.

Arjuna and his brothers attacked the palace and successfully defeated Drupada. Although Drupada had lost the battle, he was greatly impressed by Arjuna's skills as an archer.

The Pandavas held Drupada captive and brought him back to Hastinapur.

Dronacharya said with pride, 'Drupada! My brave students have brought you to me today. Here you are, like a prisoner before me. You are no more a great king and I am no more a poor man. Your kingdom is now mine! You are now left with nothing, Drupada!'

Drupada folded his hands and cried, 'Forgive me Dronacharya, for having insulted you. It was a big mistake. Now I understand that I was too proud of my power and wealth.'

Seeing Drupada repenting, Dronacharya's heart melted. He said, 'I forgive you Drupada. I will return one half of your kingdom to you. Let's be friends again.'

Drupada had learnt a lesson for being too proud and hurting his friend. Thereon, Dronacharya and Drupada became friends once again.

TITLES IN THIS SERIES

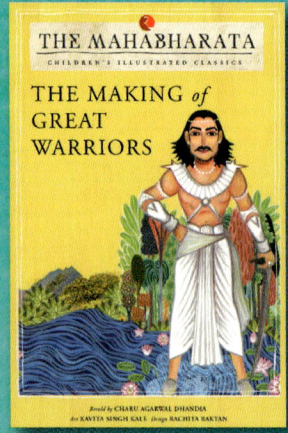
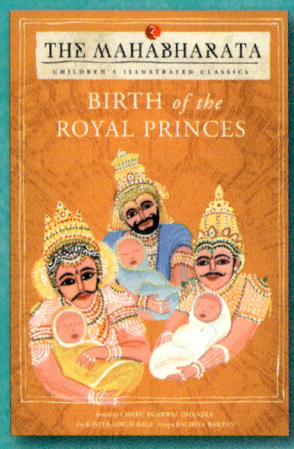
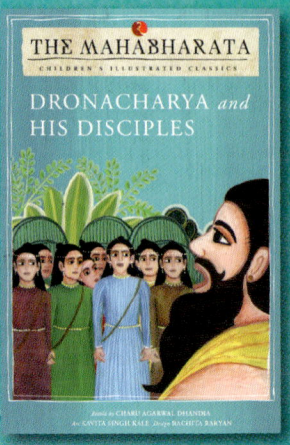
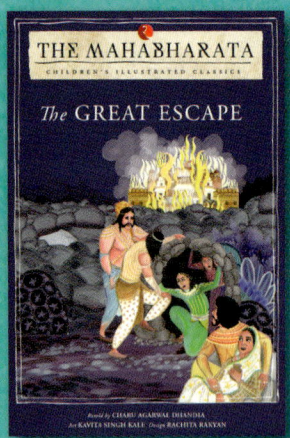
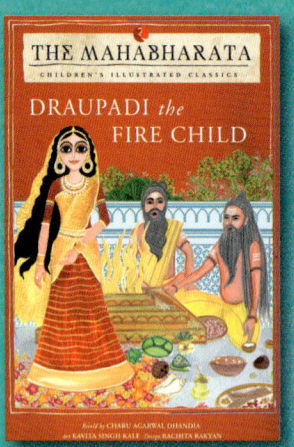
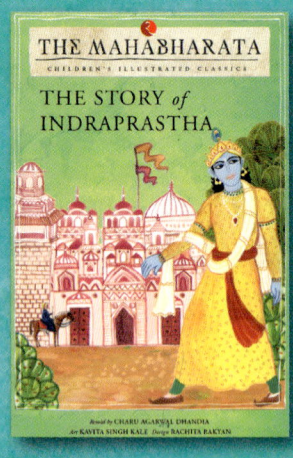
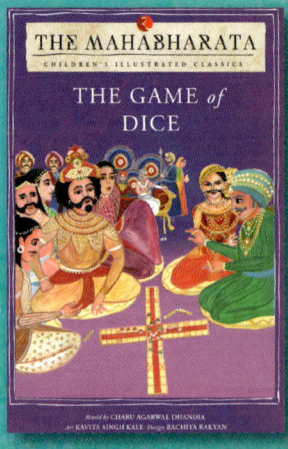
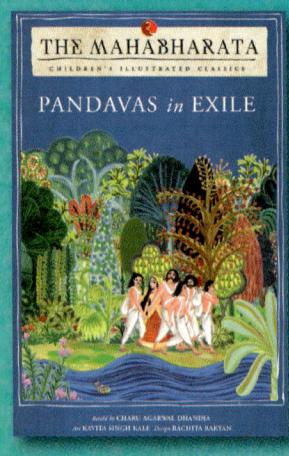
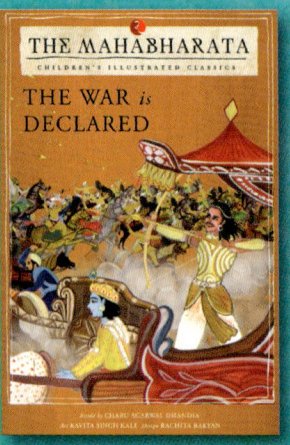